# THE ANGST IN ANARCHY

## PREQUEL NOVELLA

### TITANS OF TERRANEA
### BOOK 1.5

## NATASHA PIERCE

Pierce, Natasha

The Angst in Anarchy

Titans of Terranea #1.5

Editing and Proofreading: Under the Sea Editing

Cover Design: JG Designs

Formatting: Natasha Pierce

# BLURB

**The stars know what they are doing when they set the path for the future.**

The world of Naesala four hundred years in the past isn't much different than what we already know. The regions of the world have already been chosen and are thriving on their own. Clashes have happened in the past, however the current nations of Naesala are on the path of peace. Thus, the leaders of the world started sending their heirs to Terranea University for building political alliances.

Once I am of age and have mastered my syren's song, my father sends me to Terranea with a secret mission: to find and meet Marius Kelridge. I have to try to secure an alliance with him through a relationship in order to strengthen our kingdom. I just don't realize what a challenge this will be when angst and heartache are thrown my way. Marius is surrounded by venomous people, and he himself is arrogant and vile.

What I don't expect is meeting Felix, and then Irik. These two men stir something inside of me that I don't understand. I'm unable to stay away from both of these men despite her mission. My duty weighs on my heart, but these men lift the burden.

*When anarchy rains down around me, sides are chosen. Lines are drawn. And the fate of my future and my descendants are forever sealed.*

# AUTHOR'S NOTE

While this is a prequel, it fits into an existing series <u>after book one</u>. These characters are totally independent from the main series, **however you might miss some explanation about the world of Naesala that would have been previously explained if you have not already read The Seduction in Starlight.**

This will be an MMF story, where all of the main characters will enter into a relationship with each other.

Please note: This story was created for an anthology, and had a word limit. While I'd love to go back and add more to this story, I'm in love with the way it turned out, and I hope you will too.

# CONTENT WARNINGS

Please be aware that this story contains the following topics and kinks that some might find triggering or concerning:

Slut shaming
Graphic violence
Breath play
Edging
Piercings
Light stalking(by MMC)
On page death

# PRONUNCIATION GUIDE

**Characters:**

*Seraia Makan(Se-Ray-a Ma-Kahn), daughter of Premier Savadoe Makan(Sa-VA-Doe Ma-Kahn)
*Felix Marlowe
*Irik (Eer-ik) Whitmore
*Marius (MAR-ee-us) Kelridge
*Alya (A-Lye-a)  Caldero - daughter of dragon king Noru Caldero

**Locations:**

*Naesala(NAY-sal-uh)- Country/continent.
*Thalassia(Thuh-LAS-see-uh)- Underwater civilization for syren community.
*Terranea University- (Ter-uh-NAY-uh) secondary school for university-aged students.
*Kalakai(Kal-uh-KY) Cove- local township around the university and neighborhood.

*Kalakai (Kal-uh-KY) - region or county where this story is set.
*Myleira (MY-lee-air-uh) - Wolf shifter region.
*Fallodorn (Fal-oh-dorn) - Dragon shifter region.
*Thisavroś (Thi-sav-rose) - ancient Dragon civilization

Avallone
Tibr
Occasius River
Kalakai
Terrenea University
Belleaire Bluffs
Occasius Falls
Kalakai Cove
Thalassia
Vizcaya Pointe

MYLAERLA
EN PASS
FALLODORN
THISAVRÓS

NAESALA

SERAIA

"Fuck, I need you," Felix Marlowe whispers in my ear as we walk through the hall toward our class. "You wearing that dress has me imagining lifting it up and burying my face between your luscious thighs." His words cause heat to spread through my body, and I hesitate in denying him. "Come on, babe, I know you want an orgasm or three; I can feel your song calling out to me. Besides, you never say no."

"I hate when you show off how well you know me," I say with a smirk and an eye roll in his direction. He's right, though. Because of my elite syren heritage, I am always hungry, and I could use a top off. Begrudgingly, I allow him to pull me into a storage room off the main hall. It's not a huge space, mostly shelves for experiment supplies and extra books, but it'll work. As soon as we're inside, he shuts the door and pushes me up against it. Ohhh, is Felix feeling a certain way about dresses? I'll have to remember this for next time.

Sinking to his knees, Felix slowly runs his hands up my legs as he pushes my dress up. He groans when he reaches the apex of my thighs and sees the evidence of his dirty words left on my panties. He leans in, inhaling deeply. Fuck, I love a man willing to dive face first into my pussy.

With one quick move, Felix flips my dress over his head and then reaches for my panties. He slips them over my hips and drags them down my legs before he lifts one of my legs to throw it over his shoulder. His tongue slips between my folds, and I have to brace myself against the door and anchor a hand in his curls because it feels so good.

"Ah! Right there, fuck!" His tongue flicking against my clit builds the tension inside my body like a coil. When he reaches a finger up to stroke my opening, I shiver with anticipation. This man knows what he does to me, and in his hands, I fall into a haze of pleasure every time.

"Stop teasing me," I say, looking down at him. "You know I need you as much as you need me." He grins before he dives in again, timing the thrusts of two of his fingers with the suction of his lips around my clit. He pumps his hands and, within seconds, I feel my release gush from my core. Felix moans as he drinks all of what I give him, and when he withdraws, he pulls out from under my dress and brings his fingers to his lips.

"Fucking delicious, baby. Now, turn around. I want you from behind. But you aren't going to get us caught, are you?"

I pant as I lower my leg and spin around, eager for more of his attention. He stands behind me, and I can feel the heat of his body as he uses his large hands to knead my ass. When a loud smack lands against my cheek, it echoes through the small space, and I can't help the moan of pleasure that escapes my lips.

"Shhh, stay quiet. I know you don't want us to get in trouble. Now, spread those legs, baby. I promised you more orgasms."

He notches his dick at my entrance, and I push back, more than ready for his invasion. As he gently thrusts into my heat, I gasp. He feels so good; I can't help the low ramblings I suddenly hear myself uttering. Felix grunts as he thrusts into me, clinging to my hips for leverage. Gods, he feels so good!

As he repeatedly plunges into my heat, I can feel my orgasm building, ready to tip over again. A white-hot blaze of passion ignites in my core, and it spreads through me like a tidal wave, slow but steady, up and outward. I moan, past the point of caring who hears me. This feels too good; it always feels this way with Felix.

"Baby," he says between pants of breath, "I thought I told you to be quiet. I guess I'll have to make sure you don't get us caught." He releases one of my hips, then reaches up and wraps my long black curls around his fist. The streak of teal glows brightly in the dim light shining through the crack around the door. Once he's secured the leverage on my hair, he leans into me, pressing me against the door. He gently tugs my head back toward him, making my back arch and exposing my neck as he continues to sandwich me into the unforgiving wood. With his grip on my hair secure, his other hand snakes up, gripping my throat from behind.

"I told you I'd make sure you didn't expose us," he murmurs into my ear, and stars explode behind my eyes. The bite of pain from his hold on my hair slowly begins to throb, the sensation moving down my neck and rising to meet the wave of heat that is so close to engulfing my entire body.

I mouth the words I want to say——to scream——as bliss

explodes throughout me. I can feel my center contracting around him, my walls pulsating around his thick length and triggering his own release. He releases my throat, and I gasp for air, my chest heaving from exertion. Felix slips out of me, and right away, I feel wetness dripping down my thighs. Before I can even worry about how to clean up, he spins me around and drops to his knees again.

"I can't have you walking around uncomfortably. If I wasn't keeping these panties as a souvenir of what my words do to you, I'd make you pull them up. Let them collect my seed as it drips out of you. But I'm kind and thoughtful, so I'm going to clean you up, baby." His mischievous grin shines up at me as he ducks under my dress once more. Before I can even form a question, I feel his tongue trace up the inside of my thigh. *Gods above, this man is sinful to the core.*

Considering he promised three orgasms, Felix owns up to his words while he is under my dress. I revel in the lust he's putting off, but I also taste a different flavor. Is that a new arousal flavor from him? I push the curiosity out of my mind, and I assist Felix with straightening his clothes. When we're finally ready to leave, he stops me.

"You go out first and walk past the next lecture room. Wait for me there. I'll stay here for a few minutes." Nodding my head, I smirk at him before reaching up on my tiptoes to place a kiss on his lips. I don't linger, though, hurrying to get to our meet up spot. As soon as I close the door behind me, I feel eyes on me. I quickly scan the hallway packed with other university students. *Feeling eyes on me while in a crowded hallway, I know that sounds kind of obvious.* Even so, I am aware there is something strange in the air.

It's only after I pass the next lecture hall that I scan the students surrounding me. When my eyes lock onto a pair of deep blue eyes ignited by lust, I realize that someone actually did hear us. The tall man with thick shoulders and longer wavy blond hair is standing back near the closet door. He's so intense, and something about his stare makes me think he isn't surprised to see me here, almost like he was expecting me.

I must be lost in the flavor of his lust, now realizing this was the extra flavor I experienced earlier, and looking at him now, I feel flustered and hot. My syren is preening, basking in all the lust flowing freely around me right now. It's making me slightly dizzy. In fact, the man across the hall with heated eyes only for me is making my core clench.

Something about him draws me in, and I begin to wonder if I will ever experience his lust first hand. Felix and I have been dating casually for a while, and we obviously have great chemistry, but I don't know if it's long-term just yet. I can see myself falling for him, but I also don't feel like this is my 'perfect fit'. I was sent here for an education, yes, but also to find a suitable match. My father is pushing me to get to know Marius Kelridge, the son of a high-ranking official from the wolf community in Myleira. I guess I need to find him and get to know him, but a very persistent distraction has made that difficult.

Suddenly, Felix steps up next to me. "Baby," he whispers with a sly grin. He leans down, placing a kiss on my cheek before wrapping an arm around my waist. "Are you ready?"

"Um, I think someone heard us," I hiss into his ear. He glances around, and when his gaze locks onto the blond stranger, I can practically feel a fire between them. I watch as Felix's perusal of this new guy stokes a higher flame within me. Tugging on his arm, I lead us away. I need a breath away from this mysterious stranger.

We make it to our class and, once inside, I guide us to the far corner. I slink into a chair in the amphitheater-style room, then begin to fidget with the hem of my dress. Felix collapses beside me, a lazy grin on his face. His light hazel eyes are lit with humor, though, so I turn to him.

"What is so funny? Why are you acting like this? That guy could report us to the school. I can't get kicked out; my father would kill me!"

"Baby, whoever that guy was, he was about ready to join us. He's not going to rat us out." Felix slouches down in his chair as if it were a throne. The cocky bastard.

"What are you talking about?"

"He was into both of us, and I know he heard you. I saw a shadow pass under the door, but then it stopped and slowly backed up. I *know* you had to sense him, and I could see the way your eyes lit with interest. I mean, he was hot."

I sit there, mouth agape from his response. I don't even know what to say. As the lecture begins, I try to take notes, but I'm distracted. What did he say? Is he attracted to that guy? Am I? It seems like both hours and minutes pass, but finally the lecture ends. I pack up my notes and follow Felix out into the hall. I'm just about to say goodbye to him when someone behind me calls out.

"Marlowe! Great to see you again!" I spin to look over my shoulder, watching as a student swaggers into the building. This man seems confident, his straight, black hair causing locks to fall into his golden eyes. The man's square jawline is his dominant feature, giving him jock and playboy vibes.

"Marius, great to see you again." Felix embraces the man before turning toward me. "Seraia, this is Marius Kelridge. His father is Thomas Kelridge, a special envoy to

Kalakai from Myleira. Marius, this is Seraia Makan, daughter of Savadoe Makan, Premier of the Thalassians."

Drawing on my polite training, I extend my hand in greeting as I was trained in political and societal graces. "It's a pleasure to meet you."

Marius's smile falters as his gaze shifts to me. "Ah, yes… So, Felix. I wanted to get together for a game of Clusterball soon, now that we're both at school here."

"Yeah, um, sure," Felix responds. "We have to go, but I will catch up with you soon."

I hadn't told Felix of my dad's plans, and now I'm glad I hadn't. They are friends, and with Marius's attitude toward me, I'm just not sure how prosperous those plans will be.

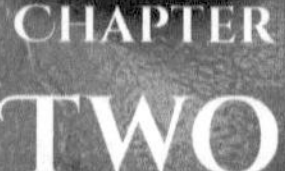

FELIX

It's been a couple days since I hooked up with Seraia. I can't get her out of my mind, but I'm trying to, at least for tonight.

My brothers and I are at the Last Call bar in Kalakai, the town outside Terranea. Samuel thinks that I need to give her up, because she's obviously meant for a family with power. Her father is our Premier, the highest leader of the underwater civilization of Thalassia. Issac, my youngest brother, thinks I should go for it, though. Who cares, it's my time to have fun. That's what he claims.

I haven't seen her since that afternoon three days ago when I left to meet Samuel for dinner. As I'm walking to class, I can feel lust rolling off of the other students in the halls, but I can't bring myself to care. Being a syren, and attending school here at Terranea has always been hard. My brothers and I are allowed to attend since my father is a professor. But we all had to manage at home until we learned how to control our powers.

Now, the lure of someone's scent of arousal makes it hard to resist. Except that my heart seems to crave only one person. My brain appears to have boarded the same crazy train, since now that's all I can focus on. Seraia. She's a goddess, really. She radiates royalty; everything about her is wrapped in charisma, style, and grace. Let's not forget that she's gorgeous, too.

"Marlowe!" I'm startled out of my thirsty daydreams by a drunken yell from down the bar. I turn, and an exasperated sigh escapes me when I notice my old friend Marius. I knew Marius Kelridge before I returned to Thalassia for my syren training. His family has always chased a higher rank in society than they could achieve, and this trickled down to Marius, too. His father has been living in Kalakai for going on ten years, so Marius and I went to secondary school together. We were Clusterball teammates, but I held him at arms' length due to the fake behaviors he always seemed to demonstrate.

"Hi, Marius," I say when I turn to greet him. "How are you doing tonight?" I assume he's feeling good, based on the amount of empty ale mugs on the bar in front of him.

"Yeah, I'm doin' good," he says, slurring his words. "We nee to hang out! We can grab an ale some time."

"Sure, let me check with my girl, and we can set a day that works."

"Ah," he says as he stumbles to his bar stool. "The bitch wit the curly hair and the teal streak? She a syren, too? Your bright green sreak is difrent." Teal hair markings have always been a sign of the royal bloodlines, so Seraia inherited it from her father, but he's in no state to understand that.

"Yes, Seraia is from Thalassia, too," I say, forcing my words through my gritted teeth. My possessiveness is breaking through, anger flooding my body as he continues.

"Ah, that stuck-up skank. She reeks of obnoxiousness," he says, taking another gulp from his mug, sloshing it over the side.

"Mm-hmm, okay. Well, I like her, so I'll be checking in with her first." I struggle to hold my temper in check with this drunk asshole who looks like he'll be sick in the morning.

"Come on, man. Wahdo you sthee in her?"

"Marius, I think she's hot. She's kind, and funny, and she's the perfect fit for me."

"I doubt that. Let me find you a girl. I know sethveral who would blow your mind, along with other things. Come on," he says, leaning on me to stand on his own two feet. "I bet I could find you a hotter girl right now."

"No. Back up, man. I don't like this version of you." I gently push him away, not wanting him to fall.

"Fuck you! Fine, go be with the trash. That's all she'll ever be. Isn't that a saying? 'You are what you eat'? Fuck, she must eat all the junk to have that big of an ass." Mairus's face turns bright red during his rant, and he can't help his heavy breathing as he climbs back up onto his stool.

"Alright man," I say, steadying him on the bar. "I'll check in next week, maybe we can still hang out." Rolling my eyes, I decide to head outside for some fresh air. I sure hope that guy is just drunk and not usually that much of a dick.

Stepping through the doors, I walk across the small patio to sit at one of the few tables. Looking across the hori-zon, I notice storm clouds in the distance. The rumble of thunder that promises a storm overnight makes me wish for the water.

I'm lost deep in my thoughts when I notice movement out of the corner of my eye. Turning, I find that blond guy who was outside the storage closet when I hooked up with Seraia. Squinting at him, I try to figure out what he's doing, then decide to call him out, letting him know I'm watching.

"I know you."

He doesn't say anything at first. He stops, for maybe five seconds, before he continues walking. He doesn't stop, not until he approaches my table. He reaches for the chair, pulling it out to sit, before he finally responds.

"You do?"

"Yeah, I've seen you before," I say.

"That's not entirely the same, though," he murmurs. His wavy blond hair hangs in front of his eyes, but the rest tucks behind his ear. Plenty of earrings dazzle in the moonlight, and I tilt my head in thought. *Is he a mage?*

"Yeah, but you were standing in the hall three days ago," I say with a smirk. "Did you like listening to me bang my girl?"

This time, he's the one with the cocky grin on his face. Damn, he's good looking. "See, I'm a mystic mage. With my mystical powers, I was able to get almost a full sensory experience."

"And what the fuck is that supposed to mean?" What is he trying to say? How could he more than hear us? He wasn't in the room.

"I could see, hear, and taste. I am able to project my aura, so I got a front row view to see and hear. But the taste... Fuck, she tastes good. I could've felt it, too, if I wanted."

"What's your point?" I'm not sure what to think about

this guy. His dark eyes hold secrets, ones I don't know won't harm Seraia.

"I sensed her when I walked up," he says with a chuckle, "but I craved you too. If I'd projected into either of you, I could've experienced what each of you felt like. Gods, that would've been something.

A sudden wave of lust washes over me as shivers run down my spine. *Who the fuck is this man?*

"Uh, yeah. I'm not sure about that," I say, hesitantly. Is he some kind of stalker?

"Sorry," he says. "I was just trying to find my new class, and I heard you. I'm sorry I eavesdropped, but seriously, you both sounded incredible. I'm glad I stuck around because your girl is delicious. Please let her know I'm not a creeper, but I had to force myself to stand there. If I moved even an inch, I might have made a move."

"I knew you were still in there, though, and I didn't want to be disrespectful." Then he leans in closer, with his elbows resting on his knees spread wide and speaks in a low voice. "I wanted to approach you first. I'm not sure how you feel about sharing your girl, but I'd love to get to know her. You too, if you're into that."

My heart races, and I slowly lick my bottom lip. Fuck, I need to talk to Seraia.

"Uh, I'm not sure. To be honest, she and I aren't... *official.*" My eyes drop, because fuck me, I don't actually have her. I want her so badly, but we've only been hooking up. Clenching my hands, I'm determined to do this. First chance I get, if I beat this guy.

"I see." With a quick motion, he hovers his phone over mine on the table. It beeps quietly, a sound I'd never heard before. He silently stands, looking down at me. Before I know it, coarse fingertips reach for me, sliding down my jaw and gripping my chin before tilting my head up. "I meant what I said. I want her. Something about her draws me in. But I want you, too."

He leans down, and I swear I imagine the briefest brush of his soft lips against mine. My pulse hammers hard in my chest, and I feel my song reach out. His arousal is sweet but mellow, in a mild white chocolate way. I wait, hoping for more, because damn. I've never felt something more tender, yet passionate.

Instead, I only get the cool night air as he walks down the road. What the fuck is going on?!

"Hey! What was that about?!" I yell out, hoping he can still hear me. "What's your name?"

He only turns, walks backward with a smirk on his face, before turning around again and continuing on. My phone dings a second later, with a new message. Fuck that, it's probably one of my brothers.

Damn. I make my way back toward the bar and pull out my phone. On the screen, I find a message from a number I don't recognize.

UNKNOWN

Don't go getting a big head or anything, but sweet dreams. Also, I can't wait to get a better taste of you, because your lips remind me of saltwater taffy. -Irik

I spin, running back out to the street. Looking out in the direction he disappeared, I'm kicking myself that I didn't say something more. At least now I have his phone number, though. And he's right, I'll for sure have some sweet dreams tonight.

# THREE



After the last time I saw Felix, I knew I had to take a break. I'm starting to catch feelings, and I don't know if he feels the same. So, I've distanced myself from him. Just taking a breather to really figure out what I want. We stayed up several nights, messaging back and forth. Honestly, I've known him for almost a year, and despite hooking up for almost the same length of time, I've been able to keep my heart protected.

When he messaged last night, I gave in since we didn't have classes today. I wouldn't have been able to put him off; he would've been pounding on my door, anyway. This man is determined to break down the walls guarding my heart, just as he could my door.

When he showed up this morning with a bouquet of flowers and a latte, I couldn't help but beam. His attention to detail, getting my latte just right, and remembering I love Myleiran Everblooms, warms my heart, and I can't help but grin as I welcome him into my apartment. I close the door with my hip, and then move to the kitchen to find a vase.

As soon as I set the bouquet down, Felix crowds in behind me, and the heat of his body against my ass sends a flutter through my heart.

"I've missed you," he whispers into my ear as he reaches around me to brace himself on the counter. "I've missed your body, yes, but I've also missed just being near you. I've been craving you near me; my heart has been spasming from withdrawals."

*Ugh.* He's so sweet. I spin in his arms, reach up to cradle his face, and pull him in for a sweet kiss. I just can't resist any more. When I pull back, I look up into his golden eyes. "I missed you."

"Next time," he says with a chuckle, "maybe don't avoid me."

"Yeah, about that..." I look away, unsure how to admit that I think I'm falling in love with him. When he suddenly pulls back and grips my shoulders, I'm startled with worry.

"What? What do you mean? Are you trying to tell me you don't want to see me again?!" The pain etched into his furrowed brows causes a pang of guilt to squeeze my heart.

"No! I promise, it's not that," I murmur. Grabbing his hand, I pull him to the sofa to sit beside me. "I-I'm a little scared to say this, so bear with me." I'm nervously wringing my hands, but once he's seated beside me, he almost instantly reaches out to hold them. Taking a breath, I continue. "I decided I needed some space. I was feeling really comfortable with you always by my side, and... I was beginning to feel things."

When the potent silence follows my admission, I glance up at Felix. I'm not expecting the huge grin across his face, though. This time, my brows wrinkle in confusion. "What?" I ask.

"I was so hurt because I feel the same way," he says, reassuring me with a gentle peck from his soft lips before pulling me into snuggle. I've missed you so much, and I'm just glad to finally have you in my arms again."

I lie there with him all morning, enjoying my latte as we catch up. It's not long, though, before he says something that catches my attention.

"So, yeah, remember that blond guy hanging around the hallway when we hooked up in the storage room? He, um, found me at the bar one night last week."

"Oh?" My eyes practically pop out of my head, because *what is this?!*

"Yeah, he, um... he said he thought we're both hot. That he had to restrain himself because he projected and found us... and mystically joined in."

"What?! Oh my gods, what the fuck does that mean?"

"Baby," Felix says, chuckling, "he's infatuated with you. He wants to formally meet you, maybe hang out. Get to know you. He's drawn to you just like I am."

"Oh," I say as heat floods my cheeks. I feel a rumble escape Felix's chest when I lean back against him, which brings a smirk to my lips. "I guess that's... nice."

"Ah, you're being a brat, aren't you? You like the idea of another man wanting you. Wanting what's mine. Are you considering what it would be like in that pretty head of yours? Curious what his lips would feel like on your collarbone?" Emphasizing his words, he bends down to graze the curve of my neck. "Do you wonder how hard his dick would be if he ground against your ass?" The thick ridge in Felix's lounge pants suddenly slots right in between my cheeks, sliding up and down, telling me just how aroused he is.

"Ah, yeah, I am now." I barely get the words out between my fast breaths.

With a sudden jerk and spin, I'm now sitting in Felix's lap, backward with my legs spread wide. I gasp, both startled and turned on at the new position. Heat surges through my veins, settling low in my stomach. Felix circles my waist with his hand, splaying it against my belly and then softly sliding it up the center of my body. When he reaches my neck and lightly grabs my throat, my nipples harden, begging for attention through my thin tunic.

"You know what I'm thinking about?" he rasps into my ear, the gritty words sinking straight to my core.

"No," I pant out, barely containing a whimper at Felix's new attitude. Where did this aggressive, domineering act come from? I'm melting because of how hot it is.

"I'm curious who can make you come faster." His hand slides up under the long hem of my shirt. "Or come harder." He hooks two fingers in my panties and yanks, ripping one side wide open. "Or how many orgasms we could wring from your body if we played together." He slowly guides his hand over my thigh, the rough pads of his fingers scorching a trail across my skin.

"Felix," I whine, not quite sure what I want. All I know is I want him to keep going. I want him to keep speaking dirty words, promising debauchery and pleasure. Clenching around nothing, I arch into his hand, begging for his touch in the one place I *need* it.

"Yeah, baby?" he murmurs. He nips at my earlobe before squeezing my neck a little harder. Fuck, what is it about his hand controlling me that has me gushing all over his pants? My thighs are fucking dripping from his teasing words. A fact he quickly discovers as his finger slides through the apex of my core, slipping through my folds with ease. His huff of laughter against my ear sends chills down my spine, and I squirm with need.

"Please." I can't do anything but beg.

"Please, what? Wait, I bet I know what you are begging for." He reaches behind me, pulling the band of his pants down far enough to pull out his dick and, in one motion, he lines up with my entrance and thrusts, fully seating himself inside me.

I gasp, the hand around my neck tightening once more. Fuck, the way he fills me, and the sensation of his cock throbbing inside me drives me wild. I arch against him again, wriggling to find some sort of friction.

"Is this what you want, baby? Ah, maybe part of it, but my dirty girl needs more, doesn't she? You aren't satisfied with just my dick, huh? That's okay. I'll just use my fingers as tools until we can find a true team player. Let's see how fast I can make you cream all over me."

Reaching his hand up and around my hip and belly, he quickly finds my clit, dragging his rough finger in slow, tight circles. I'm vibrating with need, still held within his grip around my neck. Moving my hands, I brace myself on his hips and hang on. Whatever he has planned, I know I'm not ready.

And when he begins to pump his hips, I'm gone; deceased. This isn't like our normal hookups, and something about this new guy, Irik, has him fired up and possessive. Competitive, even.

Within moments, Felix has me back on the edge, and it's like he knows my body better than I do because he holds me there. Building me up, but not letting me tip over into bliss. I'm beginning to get frustrated, but then his grip on my neck tightens, cutting off all circulation as he increases the speed of his fingers circling my clit. His thrusts increase as well, and all the sensations across my body culminate in an explosion, my syren song bursting from my body in a wave of power.

I'm buzzing with energy and drunk with pleasure, when I find myself lying on my bed. My head lolls to the side; my eyes are fuzzy but strain to find Felix.

"Shh, baby, I'm right here." His words come from in front of me, between my legs. When my gaze finds his, his golden orbs hold me captive as his tongue swipes up my core. He doesn't stop, though, his tongue tracing over and up my curves as he begins to climb up from between my thighs. He continues his trek with his tongue up my ribs, pausing at each hard peak to circle and lave with care.

Picking up his mission, Felix drags his tongue up the top of my chest, tracing up the centerline of my neck and dragging my consciousness back with force.

I lie there for a moment, trying to catch my breath. My eyes flash to his when I realize he didn't come when I did. He only smirks before positioning himself on his knees, my thick thighs draped over his. Staring down at me, he grips his cock and slowly and languidly pumps.

"This time, when I make you come, I'll join you in the stars. Baby, you're always going to be mine, no matter who else we choose to play with. You'll always own my heart."

Notching himself at my entrance, Felix slowly slides in again. His eyes roll back as ecstasy floods his body. He drops his hands to the bed, and as he begins to raise and pump his hips, a throb, warm and heavy, beats inside me. It grows, pounding within me as Felix increases the speed of his thrusts. More. Faster. The sensation builds until my skin is warm and tingling, and my heart beats hard like a war drum.

As he gets close, I can feel his dick swell, getting harder

with each thrust. I bring my hands to his shoulders and grab on tight, because when he moves one hand to my already sensitive clit, I explode for the second time. This time, light flashes out around me. Warmth spreads across my stomach, almost hot like a burn, but I can't focus on it.

I hear Felix roar from within the light that surrounds us, and his song rolls over me like a tidal wave, prolonging my pleasure. We both slow our grinding against each other until we're still. At some point, Felix rolls over onto his back.

It takes about five seconds before the fog clears, and I roll to him, my eyes wide.

"Was that—?"

"I think so," he says reverently. His eyes dip low, like he's almost ashamed. "Are you... okay with that?"

The pain in his voice has me instantly moving in to capture his plump lips with mine. That connection—the one that allows me to feel my mate's heart—immediately puts my own at rest.

"Yes, Felix," I say with a smile against his lips. "I'm happy the stars chose us for each other."

When he pulls back, I blink as I bask in the glow of orgasms from my new mate. He stares back at me, and I can feel something is still bothering him.

"What is it?"

"Now that we are fated forever, what did you want to do about Irik?" His words are thoughtful and nonjudgmental.

I lie there for a moment before he continues. "I guess it wouldn't hurt if we continued as planned." When I meet his eyes, neither of us can hold back a grin.

"I'd like that. I think you favor that option, too, huh?" I tease and wrap an arm around his waist to lay my head on his chest. Warmth and happiness radiate from him, and I snuggle into his glow, knowing mine is probably as comforting to him.

"Yeah," he says and laughs. "I'd still prefer to check out that option. We have our entire lives ahead of us; plenty of time to have some fun."

# FOUR

S eraia

    After last week, I feel like a new woman. Felix and I being mates was something I never expected, and now I know I won't have to deal with Marius, as my fate is sealed. The comfort in that is overwhelming, and I basked in the feeling that whole night.

    We found our mate marks that night; Felix noticed mine as I got up to shower, a swirl of shimmering gold across my stomach, which matched the warmth I felt that day when I came. It's something I've had to get used to, and it's so pretty that I want to wear crop-top shirts and proudly show it off. The problem is, I haven't told my dad yet. I'm deliberating how to tell him, because the alliance he wants with Marius's family won't be possible now.

    I never told Felix why I was sent here, and I'm glad. For now at least. It's inconsequential at the moment, so I don't feel the need to start drama. We've been stuck together like glue, cementing our new bond and learning more about each other. It's been like a honeymoon, basking in the glow of new love.

He did surprise me, though, by introducing me to Irik two days ago. Irik is so freaking hot, and he's quite abrupt, personality-wise. But I think he balances Felix and me well. We're both easy going and laid back, despite Felix's newly found need for control when we have sex. Ever since our mating, he's been even more authoritative when we hook up, but I'm not complaining.

It makes things interesting when we hang out with Irik. Today, for instance, both men have been clinging to me, claiming me. It feels interesting when Irik pulls my hand into his, or throws an arm over my shoulder, but Felix doesn't seem jealous, so I leave it be.

"Damn it," Felix says as the three of us sit together on the plaza grounds. The fields between the buildings have made for a nice common area to meet and people watch, allowing a nice, public place for us to chat and get to know each other.

"What?" I ask, wondering what's upset him.

"We're going to have to go. I can't walk you to class later, because Samuel needs my help with something." I pout, knowing my time with Felix is coming to a close for the day.

"I can walk her to class," Irik says nonchalantly.

Felix and I both spin to look at Irik. He just sits there, one knee up and the other hooked and lying flat on the grass, as he browses through his messages.

Felix turns to me, a question in his eyes. "Are you okay with that, Darling?"

I glance back at Irik, who peers over at me, his ocean colored eyes glinting with amusement. "I think that's fine," I say with a smile.

"Good. Behave," he says, smirking before leaning over and giving me a kiss.

Irik and I relax in the late morning sun until it's time for class. He stands, extending an arm to me to help me up. As we start walking, he slips an arm around my waist, pulling me into his side. I glance up, meeting his eyes and smile before nervously licking my lips. Irik's eyes track the small gesture, and a growl emanates from his chest so low only I can hear.

"What do we have here?" a familiar voice taunts from behind us. "What, my boy Felix isn't good enough that you have to go falling on other guys' dicks? Does he know you're whoring yourself out? Fuck, if that's the case, maybe I should get in line."

Marius Kelridge saunters out of the building as we walk by. I squint my eyes, trying to ignore him, but he doesn't let it go. "I mean, fuck, I knew you were a slut. Maybe I shouldn't have tried to warn Felix away. I thought you were too stuck up for him, but now I see I underestimated how wild you are. Hells, what do you say? Want to suck my dick, too?"

"Stop that, Marius. I won't allow you to let some diseased slut infect you. I'm not risking you spreading anything to me." An extremely beautiful woman steps out from behind him, looping her arm in his. Her long silvery hair flows in a sheet down her back, and her emerald green eyes glow with a scornful look. That scorn turns to shock and guilt, though, when Irik turns around to face the trouble that's followed us.

"Alya? Ah, I see. You did have someone else; I thought you were just distracted. Glad I only let you suck my dick. That reminds me, Seraia, I guess after I drop you off, I should go to the healers and make sure she didn't infect me. Who knows? Supposedly, people who slut around carry diseases." I turn in shock at Irik's biting words; not because he confessed to being with this girl but the vitriol in his voice. I've only known him a few days, but it appears he has some animosity toward her.

Alya, the girl with the silver hair, just scoffs as she rolls her eyes and fingers the amulet hanging against her breasts. The motion draws my eyes, and I notice the unique jewel, a nine-pointed diamond, mounted as a pendant. It's stunning, but it clashes with her cool tones. It's so sad that she doesn't realize it makes her appear drab and nearly dead.

"Whatever, Irik. Come on, Marius, stop playing with the trash." She turns and prances off, her lackluster barb falling in her wake.

"Alright," he says before turning back to face us once more. "Just tell me now. Do you swallow?" He cackles at the shock on my face before turning and following the ice bitch like a lapdog.

"Seraia, I'm sorry about that," Irik says as he gazes down at me. "If he gives you any more trouble, I want you to tell me."

"Um, okay, I guess," I reply as we turn to continue toward my class. "Why does his bully behavior bother you?"

"I was there the night Felix ran into Kelridge, and I saw his behavior then. He's toxic, on the verge of being danger-ous. And while I haven't known you long, since the day I saw you and Felix together, I've felt a piece of you in my heart. I don't want you to get hurt. I'm sorry you are now being harassed by Marius and Alya Caldero; I'll make sure they leave you alone."

As we approach my class, I face him to say goodbye, but my heart forces me to do something else. I rise on my toes, quickly placing a kiss on his soft lips. The slight rasp of stubble brushes against my chin, and the sensation sends a thrill through my body like lightning.

"Thank you for watching out for me. I appreciate the move, but I can handle myself, you know." I smile up at him, mirth hiding behind my aquamarine eyes.

"I'm sure you can, Darling." His low rumble sends a vibration through my core, and I grin at his response.

"Can I see you tonight? I'm not sure how long Felix will be occupied, and I don't want to spend it alone."

Flames alight in his gaze as thoughts of having me all to himself play out in his mind. "Of course. I have no plans tonight. Are you thinking of doing something in particular?"

My lips roll in as I try to hide my smirk. Unfortunately, I fail, and Irik sees right through me. "Ah, I see. Well, I do want to go get checked with the healers; I wasn't just saying that. If there is anything, they can catch it now. I don't trust that skank farther than I can throw her, and she's sturdier than she looks."

A giggle escapes my lips as I lean up to kiss him once more. This time, the kiss turns hot, causing an eruption to flow throughout my body. I alight with flames under my skin as his tongue sweeps across my lips. I open for him, suddenly needing more, and Irik doesn't disappoint.

We stand on the pavement outside Azure Tower, arms wrapped around each other and our tongues tangling in a lost moment of wanton energy. My inner syren flickers awake, but before things can get out of control, I grip his broad shoulders and squeeze before pulling myself away.

I smile sweetly at him, knowing he doesn't want this to end, but I have to hurry if I'm going to make my class. "Meet me outside Middleston House at eight. I'll come downstairs to escort you up."

Irik nods his head, acknowledging my statement. As I back away, I consider this strong, silent figure. Pure male, his physique is impressive, and his confidence is unmatched. I have a feeling tonight may be one of those nights that will make waves, both figuratively and physically.

# FIVE

IRIK

It's dark by the time Seraia walks outside to meet me. I've been lurking in the shadows of the trees just outside her dorm building for about two hours now. When she steps out of the door, my breath catches. She's so fucking beautiful. It was only after I watched her for a few days that I actually realized just how perfect she was, though. That was... four weeks ago? Time flies so fast.

I'm thankful I grabbed a bite to eat on the way here from the healing center. When I told them my 'girlfriend' cheated on me, they coddled me while running the necessary tests. The tears I expressed didn't hurt, either. They suggested I take things slow, and do what makes me happy. Well, that pizza I had on my way to fuck my girl makes me happy.

That bitch Ayla is lucky she didn't infect me. I don't like being crossed, and even though she didn't give me anything, she was fucking Kelridge as she tried to get me in her bed, and I won't forget that.

I stay frozen in the dark as Seraia waits for me on the steps. From my vantage in the trees, I can see she's wearing an oversized sweater, but not much else. The woman better be wearing something underneath; nevermind, it doesn't matter. The illusion is there, and if anyone else saw her, they'd imagine her full, round ass bare underneath. She's going to have to cover herself up; I'll mention something when I get her back behind her dorm room door.

Stepping out of the trees, I make my way up the path leading to Middleston House. I'm not far from the entrance when Seraia looks up from her phone to see me. The beaming smile she greets me with brings me to react in kind, something I'm not known to do often. There is something about her that draws me out of my cave of solitude that I usually retreat into. I'm not sad about it, either; being in the bright world isn't so bad when I'm with her.

"Hi," she whispers as she bounds down the steps to meet me. She wraps her arms around my neck, and my hands instantly gravitate to her hips. Her sweater rides up, and I can feel a pair of skimpy shorts, but I know they don't cover her ass. If it wouldn't draw more attention, I'd throw her over my shoulder and haul her upstairs. I'm still in my head about her ass on display when her smile comes into focus, and she leans up on her toes to kiss my cheek. "I've missed you today. Felix called; he said he won't be back till later. He's jealous I'll get to spend time with you."

As she backs away, pulling my hand along, I can't help but be curious. "He said he's jealous of me?"

"No," she says as she climbs the stairs. "He's jealous of me. That I get to be with *you*."

My eyes widen at his brazenness; he rarely flirts like that.

When we finally get to her dorm room, she invites me

inside without hesitation. My mind races as I take in her personal space. She keeps her room tidy, yet there are personal trinkets littering the surfaces, displaying a well-lived-in room. Looking at the desk, I find a picture of her and her parents. Then, on the dresser, I spy a journal and a small jewelry box. As I wander near the bed, Seraia walks over and runs her hands up my chest. When she bites her lip, I notice little zaps of electricity firing throughout my body. Anything this woman does, I'm a sucker for. How will I ever refrain from giving in anytime she asks something of me?

"I, uh, have something to say," she whispers. "I want you. I've been attracted to you since I found out you astral projected and slipped in while Felix and I were fucking." She looks down at her hands for a moment before peering up at me with her big turquoise eyes. "I feel left out, and I want a taste of you."

"So, I owe you? Because I snuck into Felix's body while he was fucking you? Because I've tasted your sweet cunt through him, but you haven't tasted me yet?"

"Yes."

She starts rubbing her body, lifting her sweater and slipping her loose shorts down her legs. *Fuck.* Why is she so tempting with her salacious curves and indecent clothes? Struggling to keep my composure, I hold my voice even as I respond.

"Why do you think I may agree?"

"You told Felix you were into both of us. I think it's about time we figured out our chemistry, wouldn't you say?"

"Tell you what," I say, lowering my voice, "show me. I need to see just how much you want me."

"Uh, what? How?"

"Lie down on the bed," I say, taking a seat in her desk chair. She does immediately, not questioning my command. *Fuck, she tasted so sweet on Felix's tongue.*

"Take off the sweater, but leave your panties on." Again, she follows my orders without hesitation. Her delectable breasts bounce free as she pulls her sweater over her head and tosses it aside. *Her skin felt so soft under his palms as he held on to her hips. I wonder if she'd feel the same with my hands. What about those glorious tits? They have to feel amazing under my hands and tongue."*

"Touch yourself. Over the panties." For the first time, she hesitates a moment, before slipping a hand down her belly and tracing the pattern of the lace. *Fuck, she's really into this.* I stand, reaching over my shoulder and grabbing the collar of my shirt before pulling it off. Glancing back at Seraia, I notice her eyes gliding over my exposed skin. Her little, breathy pants begin to get louder, a gentle little moan hidden away as her noises echo throughout the room. I turn, showing her the expanse of my back as I kick off my shoes and socks.

When I've finished with that minor task, I spin around to find Seraia nearly shaking from the attention she's giving her pussy. She's completely soaked her lace underwear, making the saturated material transparent to the skin underneath. "Ah, you're a needy little thing, aren't you, Darling?" *I'm just as fucking needy.* I can feel my dick getting harder with each second, and I'm sure to explode by the end of the night.

"Ah! Yes," she yells out. "Please!"

"Please what?"

"More!"

"Mmm. More, you say... You can touch your clit under your panties, but do not come." She nods her understanding, but that resolve nearly goes out the window when her finger slips between her folds. I unzip my pants, my resolve nearly on the edge as well. My dick is hard as I shimmy the clothes down my hips, kicking them off and taking a seat on the desk chair again.

I grip my length, slowly stroking up and down, allowing the light from the lamp beside her bed to glint off the piercings I have staggered down the underside. Her eyes drag down my body, catching on the jewelry I'm obviously not hiding, and her eyebrows furrow. The cute little whimper and lip bite that follows almost does me in, so I reach down and grab my balls in an attempt to restrain myself.

"There are some things I need to say before I touch you. Some things you need to know about me."

"Okay," she says, panting heavily.

"I'm obsessed with you." I wait a moment for her reaction, but she doesn't give one, so I keep going. "Add your fingers from your other hand. Slide your panties to the side and spear your cunt for me."

She does so, a low moan rolling from her lips. Her small little nipples harden, rising above the flesh of her breasts as they bounce with each motion.

"I watched you for four weeks before you caught me off guard in the hallway." Still no reaction, except now she's writhing on the bed. "Taste yourself. Taste what I tasted through Felix."

Finally, she briefly pauses once more before completing the assigned task. *Fuck, my hand feels good, but I know her dripping cunt is bound to feel even better.*

"Does it bother you? That I've known who you are, and tracked you, watched you any moment I could?"

"No, you didn't hurt me," she cries. "You have been respectful, not even touching me when I beg you to!"

"You like this though, don't you, Darling?" I say, a chuckle spilling from my lips. She begins to tremble, fighting off her impending release. I'm proud that she's resisting, the sweat beading on her brow proof of her restraint.

"I can be demanding," I say. "Controlling. Requiring you to do things how I say, when I say. I won't ever hurt you, though."

Her entire body quivers as she writhes on the bed, trying her best to do as I ask so I'll reward her.

"Can you accept that of me?"

"Yes!" Her cries reveal how close she is from her orgasm, so I have to act fast.

"Stop!" My voice echoes as she whimpers, but she does as I ask and freezes in position, not daring to move.

"What?" she breathes, turning her head to stare me down.

"Your orgasms belong to me. And Felix, if he's there. We are your completion, only us." I stand, lunging to her side on the bed. I snap her pretty lace panties on both sides and shove my head into the apex of her thighs. Swirling my tongue, I build her back up again. Finally, I slide two long, thick fingers into her center and, immediately, I can feel her walls pulsate around them. Fuck, she tastes amazing. A sweet and salty mixture that reminds me of the best trop-ical delicacies. I continue licking her, alternating with full mouth sucks until I feel her explode underneath me. A wash of warmth flows over me, and as I pull back from her, I see no evidence other than a sated syren. *Ah, that was her song. I vaguely remember that, too.*

Climbing off the bed, I stand and back up a few steps. "On your knees, Darling," I call to her. "I want to know how amazing your mouth feels before I fuck you to sleep." She tilts her head up at me, a blissed-out look in her eyes. After a moment, she rolls to the edge of the bed before sliding off and kneeling on the rug at my feet.

Peering up at me, she sticks out her tongue, waiting for me. *The little brat.* I ignore the behavior for now, but I'll be addressing this later.

As soon as my dick touches her tongue, I shiver with pleasure. Her mouth is so fucking warm and wet, just as heavenly as I knew it would be. I fold my hands behind my head for several minutes, allowing her to get used to the feel of the piercings in her mouth. I know if I touch her, I'm taking control.

Within minutes, though, I feel a stirring deep in my gut. I know I'm getting close, so I decide to cut this short. "Darling, I'm going to take over. Are you okay with me holding on to your hair?"

With her responding moan of appreciation, I collect her long black curls, carefully wrapping the long strands around my fist. Holding her gently, I slowly begin to thrust, working my way deeper into her mouth. When I finally hit the back of her throat, I groan. The feeling of her hot mouth —her tongue working me over—is giving me that static, numb feeling in my balls. It won't be long before I blow, so I need to get a hold of myself *now.*

"That's right, take my dick deep into your throat," I say as I thrust further into her mouth. I can feel the squeeze of her throat as she tries to swallow around me. "I've been waiting for this. You're just how I imagined—no, better." Fuck, she starts to gag, but I need these last few thrusts before I pull her away. She claws at my thick thighs, and when I give in and pull her off of me, she smiles and wipes her chin with the back of her hand.

"Ah, such a good girl for me, aren't you? Were you trying to make me come down your throat?"

She bites her lip, a mischievous grin spreading across her face. "Nope, I wouldn't consider that. Not on our first night together, at least."

I growl with frustration, leaning down and sweeping Seraia off the floor and into my arms. Within moments, though, I'm tossing her onto the bed and sliding onto the mattress behind her. Reaching my arm around her, I pull her head to the side, fiercely attacking her lips in a passionate kiss. This woman drives me crazy, in the best and worst ways; I guess she has the excuse that it's not far of a drive, though.

Breaking the kiss, I lift her leg up and over my hip. "Can I finally fuck you before you cause me to embarrass myself?" Tilting my hips, I thrust through her soaked core, waiting for her to say the word.

"Yes, please. Fuck me, Irik." Without hesitation, I find her center and thrust deep. Her gasp rattles through my ears, and I turn her shoulders so her lips are within reach. I swallow her moan as I begin to move my hips. Wrapping my arm around her shoulders, I grip her neck, but only hard enough to hold her to me.

"Yes! Oh my gods, right there. Fuck. Right there!" Her screams are loud, and I don't care if they wake anyone else. I'm making my girl come so hard, she'll fall asleep in my arms, right where she belongs.

Turning into her side only slightly, I whisper into her ear, "You like that, Darling? Do you like clamping down on my cock while I rail you from behind?" She only moans a response, and my mind goes blank as I start to pump into her pussy. Fuck, the only thing I know is a warm, wet cunt attached to the woman with the body of a goddess.

I feel nothing but pure bliss rolling through my body until she flutters around my dick, and I yell, coming hard. Her moans fill the space, and I collapse with her in my arms. After a moment, I check in with her.

"Are you okay? Was that too much?"

"No," she replies, a soft smile warming her voice.

"Good," I say. "Because even though you and Felix are mated, I choose you both."

SERAIA

Two days have passed since the night with Irik. Things have been so nice, and he and Felix have been so caring and attentive. They rarely leave me by myself, but I'm enjoying having them around. It's been funny to watch them flirt awkwardly because they haven't found a way to voice their feelings, audibly or physically.

I brought it up to Felix this morning, but he kind of sidestepped the conversation, so I waited until we were at the gym to bring it up again.

"So, um, when did you plan on pushing things with Irik? I'm totally supportive of this; you should find some time with him," I say as we switch back to the treadmills to cool down.

"Ah, I, uh," he stutters as we start the speed higher to cool ourselves down slowly, "I'm not sure. The opportunity just hasn't arisen because that needs to be slightly private, you know?"

"Yeah, I get that," I say, my voice trailing off. I feel a

little guilty because the guys have been sticking to my side like glue. We continue the cool down process in a comfortable silence, and I contemplate how I can get them time to themselves. It's hard when people seem to hate me now. To be honest, the only time I've had to myself recently is when I'm asleep.

"Are you done?" Felix's question breaks me out of my hyper focus, alerting me to his dismount of the treadmill.

"Yeah, I'm done," I reply, flashing a smile. We walk toward the locker rooms to grab our things, and I reach out, grabbing his arm at the last second before he turns into the men's room. "Hey. I may head straight home. I think I want some quiet time and to clean my dorm."

"You sure?" he asks. "I can walk you home."

"I'm good, I promise," I say, beaming at him to put him at ease. He's just trying to protect me. "I'll message you later to see what you're up to once I figure out the chaos brewing at home."

"Alright, baby. I love you." He smiles before leaning down, placing a gentle kiss on my cheek.

"Bye!" I grin before spinning around and jogging into the locker room. I use the restroom, then head to the sink to wash my hands. When I glance up into the mirror, I find Alya standing behind me, looking pissed off.

"Uh, hi," I say, trying to be polite. "Can I help you?"

"Yeah, skank, you can leave," she hisses.

"Alright, I was just leaving," I say, rolling my eyes in exasperation. *Damn,* she's insufferable. I turn off the water and turn to leave when Alya pushes me back, bending me over the counter.

"Bitch, I didn't mean the locker room. I meant the school. You are trash, and don't meet the quality Terranea is known for. I can't believe either of those two idiots fell for you, but you can whore yourself out elsewhere."

"What the fuck are you talking about?" I am pissed and so confused at this point.

"Everyone knows you are mated to Felix Marlowe. We can see his mate marks, and he's only been sniffing around your ass for weeks. Congratu-fucking-lations. Except the problem is, our entire floor in Middleston House heard you screaming Irik Whitmore's name two nights ago! Normally, I would say 'get yours, girl', but your whoring around is blatant and disruptive. So either shut your mouth or stop cheating on your mate!"

My cheeks instantly flame at the realization that I was loud enough while having sex that others heard me. I'm going to have to figure out a spell to soundproof my room, preventing people from being nosy.

"You don't know what you're talking about. That's not what's going on," I say.

"All I know is that I heard you fucking someone else four days after your mate mark shows itself," she snipes back. "People probably wouldn't question it, had you not shown it off over the weekend when you were hanging over Felix where everyone could see!"

"You've got it all wrong. Listen to me. I'm not cheating on Felix!"

"Why should I listen to you? You're a lying fucking whore!" Her face begins to turn red and splotchy as she continues to yell.

My eyes pool as I struggle to fight off this emotional attack. Why does this bother her so much? Why does my life matter to her? Just as I'm stuttering to come up with a response, a figure appears over her shoulder. I blink away the tears, only to focus on Irik standing behind Alya. My eyes bulge, as he's in the women's locker room.

"What's wrong, little whore?" she asks, grabbing a hold of my shoulders and shaking me. "There aren't any dicks for you to stuff your mouth with in here, are there? Is that the problem? You don't know what your mouth feels like without a dick in it?"

"You're one to talk, aren't you?" Irik says, sliding a dagger over her shoulder and holding it to her throat. Her gasp echoes through the room as her hold on me lessens. "So here's what's going to happen. You're going to take your hands off of Seraia." He pauses, waiting for Alya to comply. Once she drops her hands, he continues.

"Now, you will walk out of here. You will not come at my girl again, no matter the reason. If you can't abide by that rule, you'll have to face the consequences, like any other petulant child throwing a tantrum. Are you capable of understanding this new rule?"

Alya goes to nod her head, but the movement pulls at her neck and she winces. "Yes," she shakily replies. When Irik leans in to whisper in her ear, I strain to hear his words. He, unfortunately, keeps his murmurs to himself and Alya, despite locking his eyes with mine. He says something too quietly for me to hear, and she visibly gulps before replying.

"Ye-yessir," she stutters, trying to gain control of her tongue.

"Just in case the question arises, I feel you should know. I can get through any locked door on campus. If you doubt me, you know how to test my abilities." He slowly drags the tip of the dagger down her throat until he reaches her collarbone. He then drags it up and over her shoulder before shooing her away.

As she runs whimpering from the locker room, Irik

inspects his dagger, turning it over in his hands as if to see if she soiled the gleaming metal with her dirty blood. I finally push myself upright, standing on my own two feet. As I regain control of my posture, Irik turns to me.

"Are you alright?" His suspicious gaze skims over my body, as if to check for himself.

"Yes, she barely touched me. Thank you, she just caught me off guard; I'd only just left Felix," I say, my voice slightly shaky from the experience. Fuck, that startled me a bit more than I'd prefer.

"I know," he says nonchalantly. "I was watching from across the weight room. You hadn't left him thirty seconds before she stormed in. I was waiting, because I knew that bitch was up to something. I doubt she'll leave you alone, but that's okay. She'll soon find out I'm not someone to fuck around with." Meeting my eyes once more, he smiles and checks in with me. "Well, did you need an escort home?"

Seeing his true nature after his confessions the other night is slightly alarming, but I was truthful with how I felt. I know he won't hurt me, and he seems to be fiercely protective of me. Which I'm all for when crazy bitches on a power trip want to come after me.

"I should be fine, now that you've claimed me. Thank you," I say with a smile. There is something about his mind that is scary yet comforting.

He leans down, taking my lips with his and grasping a hold of my waist before tugging me against him. My hands instinctively rest on his powerful chest, and tingles spread through my body as his tongue demands entrance through my lips. I give in, opening for him, and he hums as he swirls his tongue around mine. Heat builds inside my stomach once more, but this time it is from desire instead of physical exertion.

When he finally pulls back, I pant, and a chill runs down my spine. He nods as if he's fulfilled his purpose and then backs away with a smirk.

*Fucker!* He knew how he left me. I glare at him, returning his smile, because I'm sure he's just as aroused. That's okay, I'm sure I'll see him later, and I plan on returning the favor.

# SEVEN

FELIX

I did not expect to see Irik sneaking into the women's locker room as I left the gym. I also didn't expect to see Alya Caldero cornering our girl, but the biggest surprise was Irik threatening her with a dagger that looked incredibly dangerous. Irik gives off the psychotic, deadly vibe, but I never expected this severe of a reaction. Alya has been harassing Seraia for no fucking reason.

When I saw Irik draw the dagger, I backed away, not wanting to witness something more than I was ready for. I waited outside the gym, unsure of what to expect. I certainly didn't expect Alya to run out, look both ways, and then continue calmly on her way. Confused, I make my way back inside the gym, but after waiting by the locker rooms for them, it seems I have missed both Irik and Seraia.

Fully trusting Irik with Seraia, I'm not worried that he'd hurt her. So, I decide to give Seraia the space she asked for, considering she appears safe, for now. I message Irik, trying to track him down.

> Hey, where are you?

IRIK

> I'm on my way back to my dorm.

> Which room? I need to see you.

IRIK

> 309, Bromberg House.

I set out, determined to get answers about my mate. When I finally reach his room, my heavy knock echoes through the hall. When he opens the door, his perusal of my body is unmistakable but unexpected.

"Hey," he says, his eyebrows jumping with amusement at my obvious urgency. "Come in. I assume you rushed over here for something specific?" He opens the door wider, motioning me to enter his apartment. Walking past him, his scent of warm honey and whiskey stirs something in my bones. My dick decides to wake up to the idea that Irik probably tastes the same.

I glance around his apartment, taking in his environment. It's clean, almost sterile, but with just enough touches of comfort that seem just like him. I'm so distracted with being in his space that I don't hear him close the door, or even approach me from behind. When he gently slips the straps of my satchel from my shoulders and drops it to the floor, I shiver from the graze of his fingertips down my arms.

"What is so important that you had to rush over here and invade my space?" His deep words rumble over my shoulder as he steps into my back. I'm not a short man by any means, but Irik towers an extra four inches over me. His heavy breath ghosts over my neck, the warmth causing goosebumps to erupt over my arms.

Needing to see his eyes when I say the words, I spin, only to have him advance, backing me up against his desk. His unexpected aggressiveness steals my breath, and my mind blanks on the words to answer him. When my dick begins to harden against him, he smirks at my reaction. Only, I can feel him hardening against my thigh as well.

"Answer me," he says, leaning over me and bracing both hands on the desk on either side of me.

"Yes, sir," I reply shakily. My mind races with the possibilities of what will happen next. "Um, I, uh, I saw what happened at the gym. I saw you threaten Alya, and I'm glad you did. That bitch waited until Seraia was alone, and that fucking pisses me off. I'm thankful you were there. So yeah, I wanted to thank you. Though, I know you care for Seraia and wouldn't let anything happen to her. I know you're possessive and, well, I'm just glad you were there."

"Will you stop rambling long enough for me to kiss you?" As soon as I hear his words, confusion washes over me, and within a split second, Irik's lips descend on mine. My hands work up his back, clinging to him through the gravity that is his kiss. I never expected this sort of reaction to someone I'm not fated to, but I'm ready.

When he interrupts the kiss, he stares deep into my eyes. "Are you ready to break through this stalemate we've had? I want you, and by the feel of things," he says, grinding his rock hard dick against mine, "you want me, too."

"Fuck," I breathe. This man shatters my hesitation with each word uttered from his mouth.

"That's the point, Handsome."

His devilish smirk only adds to the haze of lust emanating from him, and I lick my lips at his warm and woodsy flavor. "What did you have in mind?"

"Are you up for fucking my ass?" My eyes bulge at the

thought. I hadn't yet considered that a thing, and now that I'm thinking about it, I know I want to, but I'm just not sure I can today. "It's okay. How about you suck my dick for now? See how things go?"

I nod furiously as Irik stands upright, pulling his shirt over his head. I drop to my knees, my hands migrating up his legs toward the drawstring of his pants. As my hand glides over his obvious bulge, I swallow. *Fuck.* I'm large, but he's fucking huge.

I pull the string loose and tug his pants down, allowing his cock to pop free from the restraints. *Oh my fucking gods.* With his dick erect and at eye level, I can see that not only is he, in fact, larger than me, but he has piercings down the underside. Nine individual bars line up in a ladder from the tip to the base. I panic slightly when I think about how they will feel in my mouth. Will I have to be more careful?

"You can do it. Seraia did," he teases, his smirk returning to his lips with his amusement at my hesitation. My eyebrows jump, and my dick goes incredibly hard. *Seraia took that into her small mouth?* She struggles with me. I guess I can't back out for that reason alone then.

As soon as the thought crosses my mind, I throw it out. Fuck quitting. Fuck it in its gaping ass. I'm going to swallow his cock like a champ. Taking it in my hand, I reach down with the other to adjust my dick. Gods, it is throbbing right now, aching with need. Guiding Irik's dick to my mouth, I pause for only a second before wrapping my lips around him.

His groan floats down to my ears as Irik rests a hand on the back of my head. I work on slowly taking as much of his length into my mouth as I can while remembering to pay attention to his piercings. The metal warms from my tongue, and I trace around each barbell, one at a time.

It doesn't take long for Irik to become impatient, and even though he knows I'm ready, he's holding back. He's not the most stable of people, so knowing this and the fact that he hasn't disregarded my hesitations, means he must really care about me.

"Fuck, Felix, you're such a fucking cock tease, aren't you? Your mouth feels so good. Fuck it," he says before pulling me off of him and spinning around. In one fluid motion, he swipes everything off his desk, including the lamp. Reaching into a drawer, he pulls out a small bottle. "Get your ass up here and bend over the desk. I want to get you ready for me. You may not be ready to take me, but I need you. Now."

My eyes bulge, but I jump to my feet. I hurriedly strip off my shirt, then drop my shorts and lean over the desk. I'm so fucking nervous, but I know he cares for me, so I do my best to relax.

It's only moments after I hear the click of a cap that I feel the cool liquid drip between my ass. A shiver runs down my spine at the unfamiliar sensation. I'm so uptight I nearly jump out of my skin when Irik softly grazes my shoulder before gently running his hand down my back.

"I won't hurt you, I promise. I'm going to warm you up a little. Relax you a bit." I nod in understanding, doing my best to relax. "Spread your legs a little, Handsome."

Widening my stance has me focusing on the positioning of my feet when suddenly a warm hand cups my balls. My mind short circuits, and I freeze, unable to say or do anything as he has found my weakness. The slow, tender caress has my dick incredibly hard, but while I'm lying with my chest flat on the desk, I'm unable to do anything to relieve the tension.

While I'm concentrating on the heavenly feeling

surrounding my balls, a fingertip ghosts over my entrance. I clench in shock, but with the repetitive movements, I eventually relax into his touch. He gently puts more and more pressure until he slips his finger inside. I gasp, shocked at how good it feels.

"That's it. Let me slip another finger in." I release the tension in my shoulders and will the rest of my body to relax. When that second finger slips through, a sharp jolt flares through me before ebbing away. "Right there. Hold on, I'm going to stretch you for me."

The next few minutes are uncomfortable, yet still have me rock-fucking-hard. I finally release a full breath when he withdraws his fingers, but that gives me only a second of relief. When I feel the blunt tip of his dick nudge against me, I instinctively clench. It's only when Irik rubs my back while trying to notch himself that I manage to shut my mind down.

That very moment he begins to thrust, little by little, is the culmination of all of my anxieties since I met him. It builds as the tension in my ring of muscles gets tight, but then everything—I mean everything—slips away into nothing once he's inside of me.

"Gods damnit, Felix, you feel so tight and warm." I'm speechless, unable to respond. All I know is that Irik adds more lube as he begins to sink deeper into me. Thrust after thrust, he works his way in, going slowly to not injure either of us with the steel bars lining his cock. When he finally sinks so deep that his hips touch my ass, I moan.

"Fuck!" Irik swiftly but gently withdraws from me before yanking me upright.

"What? What did I do?" I ask, shock washing over my face. I don't want to fuck this up, and that felt *sooo* good.

"You. You almost made me bust in that tight ass of

yours before I was ready. You have the tightest ass I've ever felt; it rivals how good our girl's pussy feels." My eyes widen in surprise as he continues. "I'm not coming without you, and I want to look into your fucking eyes and taste your lips as I fill you up."

Irik turns me around, allowing him to hop up on the desk and lean against the wall. He then props one leg on the desk, and the other on the armchair to the right.

"Get your ass up here and sit on my cock. I want you in my lap, so I can stroke your dick at the same time. I need to come, and I know you do, too."

"Yes sir," I say, jumping up on the desk. As I do, Irik emits a growl that sounds almost scary.

"That's right, Handsome. Sir... I like the sound of that," he purrs.

I straddle one of his legs and lean against the wall, bracing as I lower myself. When I get low enough, Irik supports my ass as I reach between my legs to grip his cock and line him up again. When he's ready, I slowly relax my thighs, lowering my body and allowing him to penetrate me once more.

"Fuck, fuck, fuck," I murmur at the blazing heat flooding my body. As he fully seats me in his lap, Irik grunts, and he swings my leg over his arm. My eyes roll with pleasure, similar to what I experience with Seraia. When he takes my dick in his hand, I moan entirely too loudly.

"You like that, don't you? You like it when I fill you up? Give me your mouth; I need to taste you." I reach my arm around, gripping the hair at the back of his neck and bringing my lips closer to his. Just as our lips meet, he starts to thrust into me, lifting us both off the desk.

"Shit. Fuck," I curse with the heat searing into my body

at his touch. He kisses me deeply, not caring whether he's too rough. He captivates my mouth, fully dominating my focus with the way he feels both inside and outside my body. It's when he starts pumping his fist around my length that I lose all control.

Shaking, I cling to Irik, unable to care about anything except my existence in this scene. He rides my ass, taking his pleasure but giving to me as well, and I am helpless to say or do anything. This feeling—connection with him—is unlike anything I've ever experienced.

"Fuck, Handsome, after the work your mouth did, I'm going to come. Are you going to come with me?"

"Yes, yes. Fuck. Fuck!" Looking deep into his eyes, I find his soul bared to me as I erupt over his hand. Just seconds later, as I shake from the exertion in his arms, Irik groans, straining as he thrusts hard into my ass, holding me close.

We sit together, slowly catching our breath and coming down from our high. "I don't know what I expected, but it wasn't that," I say, slowly standing and easing his cock from inside me. "That," I say as a turn in his arms, "I can't wait to do again."

"Let's go shower," he says, leaning in to kiss me. "If you give me five minutes while we wash each other, I know I'll be ready for round two."

"Lead the way, sir," I say, teasing him because of the reaction I got earlier.

"Don't start something you can't finish, Handsome."

"Game on," I say with a laugh as I follow Irik to the shower. "Game on."

SERAIA

The past few weeks with Felix and Irik have been blissful. We've slowly begun to learn who we are in our relationship with each other, and we've been able to experiment in the bedroom. They've been patiently working me to take them both at the same time, but with how big they both are, it's been a task to undertake.

School has been good, and I'm doing well in all my classes. I can't believe things have been so great, and I'm looking forward to meeting with an advisor at the end of this term to better plan for the future. I know I'll have to do something to prepare for my future as Premier of Thalassia, but I'm unsure of how to proceed with my education.

After deciding I want to shift today, I consider just how much my life has changed as I gather a towel and head to the pool for the afternoon. Within just a few months, I've met the mate the stars destined for me. I've also met someone I choose to be with and who chooses me as well.

Irik is... quirky. *That's one way of saying it,* I think, chuckling to myself. He's definitely protective and possessive, except with Felix. I think his relationship with Felix allows him to be in the mindset to share me with Felix, and vice versa.

I know my father still wants me to get to know Marius, hoping to build something with him, but the idea of dating that self-centered, arrogant asshole is repugnant to me. I'd never be caught attempting to show him affection. It's enough to know that I'm lucky to have found two men who treasure me so much.

I'm lost deep in thought, trying to figure out how to tell my father I could never marry someone who would treat me poorly, when I cross by the dining hall on my way to the pool house. Just as I pass the entrance path, I hear a familiar voice filled with vitriol and venom.

"There's the slut who's whoring herself around." Turning my head, I see Marius exiting the dining hall. "I thought the rumors couldn't be true, but I've been watching. I know you've mated with Marlowe, and you've been clinging to the weird-ass dude, Irik Whitmore. What, did you and Felix work together to seduce the crazy guy?"

I roll my eyes as I respond in the least confrontational way I know. "Leave me alone, Marius. What I do is none of your business," I murmur and try to walk by him.

"That's where you're wrong, princess," he says, approaching me, getting in my face. "My father told me your father talked to him about a potential marriage between us. Seems you didn't tell your father you mated with someone from his kingdom, did you?"

Marius's face begins to flush as he waits for the answer I'm unable to admit. *Fuck*, this happened faster than I imagined. Yeah, I hadn't told my father I'd found my mate, but I never imagined he would go around me to talk to Marius's father. And now that Father has already started the talks with Mr. Kelridge, I can't explain that I've mated another syren, let alone someone of lesser rank in our society. It could risk a lot, potentially even Felix's life.

What does that matter now? It's not like I have any choice in this anymore.

"The thought of having to fuck you until you give me a child makes me sick. You are revolting, even on the best of days. Not to mention I don't want to marry the school whore."

"That's okay, Marius. At least she knows how to spread her legs," Alya says, stepping up beside him. "She's just practicing for when you take her as your wife. Don't worry, babe, I'll be there for you when you want to be treated like a king."

"Shut up," I retort. "What interest do you have in this situation? Or are you just being a nosey bitch again?"

"When you marry Marius, I'll be his mistress until he can get rid of you," she snipes back. "Unfortunately, this will be years later, when he can have you kicked out for all you've done to him."

"Fuck that," I say, turning to Marius. "I'm not marrying you."

"I'm not happy either, bitch. But for my family to survive, I have to marry you. Even though we look elite in the Myleiran Wolf community, we've struggled as of late. My father convinced me to take you as a wife and put a baby in your fat belly. After that, I don't fucking care, so long as I'm not disgraced."

No way. No *fucking* way. I will never sleep with this gods-awful dickhead. I'd rather die than lie in bed with him. How would I even marry him? Live in the same house?

"What, you afraid of a little sex?" he says, snarling and

exposing his teeth. "It's nothing you haven't been practicing for, slut. Whoring yourself around seems to be your newfound profession. Surprised we haven't caught you with more people."

"Oh, Marius," Alya interjects again, "make sure and get her tested for diseases before you touch her. I don't want her giving you anything that you could spread to me." Gods, she is a complete bitch.

"I thought you were told to leave me alone? What is your obsession with me anyway?" I can't help but spit the words at her, my patience finally wasting away. I've done everything I can to ignore her foulness, but I'm done being the mat she walks all over.

"I just find it hard to believe that so many men are falling over themselves for your fat ass," she says, turning her nose up and inspecting her fingernails. "Your mouth and ass must feel good because when you're on your knees or bent over, at least they don't have to look at your flabby belly or ugly face."

"You're one to talk. You have no tits or ass to speak of, no wonder Irik ran as fast as he could from you."

"You fucking bitch!" Alya screeches before lunging at me, her claws held high. Unfortunately, I don't have time to defend myself since she was only a few steps away. Her sharp manicure grabs at my hair, latching on and ripping. Luckily, she couldn't rip the hair completely out, but she did manage to drag her nails down my face.

I let out a pained scream, attempting to block anymore of her attacks. When I can blink enough to clear my vision, Marius watches with a smirk as she continues to pull my hair and claw at me. Fine, bitch, let's play.

With all the fury I feel from her harassment fueling me, I wind up and punch her. Her nose explodes, dripping with blood dark like ink, but I don't relent. I throw a hooked fist toward her cheek, which knocks her to her knees. I'm just about to start kicking the shit out of her when Marius steps in, blocking her from my attack.

"Control yourself, Seraia," he says, eyes glowering at me like dark, soulless pits.

"She came at me! Why the fuck should I control myself?" I spit back at him.

Marius catches me completely by surprise with a swift palm strike to my cheek. The pain from the power behind his hit washed over me as if I was being doused in boiling oil. The force was so hard; I was knocked off my feet. I don't even realize what just happened until I blink, tilting my head back to look at him towering over me.

"Watch your mouth. If you can't control yourself, you will find that once we are married I will force your obedience." A look of shock must be the mask my subconscious has chosen to wear as a reaction because he only sneers. "Get used to it. Any time you step out of line between now and then, you'll learn your lesson of what I expect from my wife."

"Keep your slutting to a minimum. At least, behind closed doors because I'm going to have to claim you publicly soon." His rage fades into a look of disgust as he peers down at me, spewing such hateful and degrading words. "Such a fucking disappointment. And a waste of a wife. I could have had anyone, and Father chose you."

He sucks at his teeth as he turns his back on me, bending to pick Alya up, cradling her in his arms. Alya starts her 'poor me' act, instantly bursting into tears and whining to Marius.

"How could you let her do that?" she cries as Marius carries her off. "She broke my nose! She's lucky she didn't break my amulet. You need to do something about her, Marius. You can't let her get away with that!" Her screechy voice begins to fade as they walk off toward the healing center. It doesn't matter that she jumped me, or that Marius nearly launched me across the courtyard here near the dining hall. Alya is the spoiled princess everyone makes her out to be, and Marius only feeds her narcissism.

Picking myself up, I continue on the way to the pool. Shifting will help the healing process, but between the scratches down one side of my face and the swelling that is already forming from Marius's swing, I'm sure I'll go home with marks of some kind. I just hope I can hide them, so Irik doesn't react. If he finds out, all the fury of the fates won't be enough to protect those two.

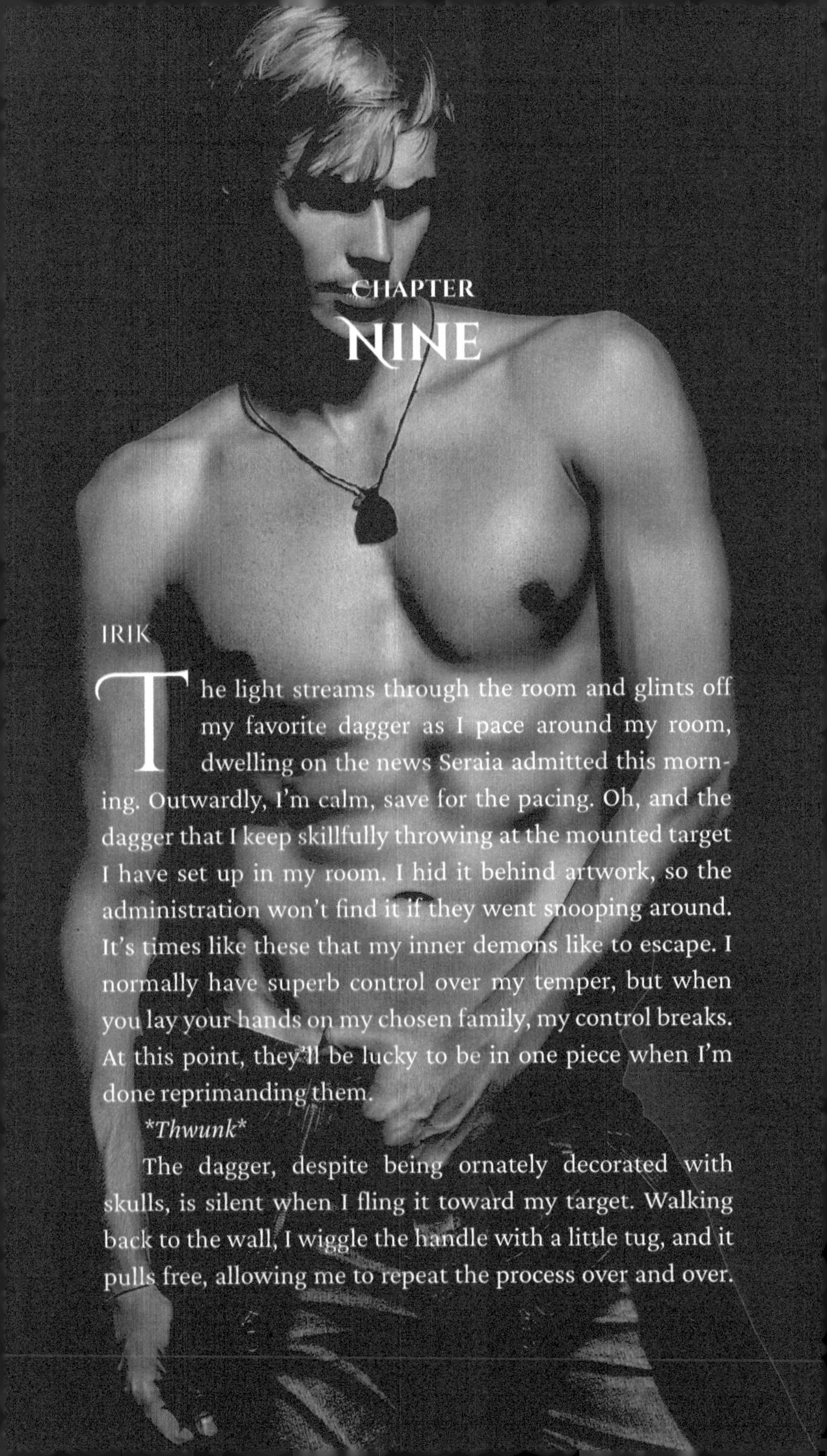

IRIK

The light streams through the room and glints off my favorite dagger as I pace around my room, dwelling on the news Seraia admitted this morning. Outwardly, I'm calm, save for the pacing. Oh, and the dagger that I keep skillfully throwing at the mounted target I have set up in my room. I hid it behind artwork, so the administration won't find it if they went snooping around. It's times like these that my inner demons like to escape. I normally have superb control over my temper, but when you lay your hands on my chosen family, my control breaks. At this point, they'll be lucky to be in one piece when I'm done reprimanding them.

*Thwunk*

The dagger, despite being ornately decorated with skulls, is silent when I fling it toward my target. Walking back to the wall, I wiggle the handle with a little tug, and it pulls free, allowing me to repeat the process over and over.

As I circle the room, lost in my thoughts, I recap the time I've known Seraia.

The very first time I saw her, I was in the weight room in the athletic center, walking to the locker rooms. Seeing her swim in the giant pool in her shifted form had mesmerized me. But watching her shift back and slip on her bathing suit before climbing out of that pool... I was hooked. She reeled me in, without even knowing, and her spell wrapped around my heart. I followed her from a distance for weeks, saw her meet Felix and slowly begin to trust him enough for a date. At that point, I was jealous of them both.

Then I happened to be walking down the hall after class one day when I spotted her. Seraia. I learned her name after the first week, and it's the only name I can utter anymore.

*Thwunk*

Pacing around the room, I consider the situation. I already threatened Alya with violence, but the tag team they unleashed on her deserves something more than a beating. Simple violence is no longer enough; they deserve every ounce of effort I can use to make them miserable.

I wonder if Marius could deal with a little disfigurement during the night?

*Thwunk*

My jaw begins to hurt from the tension radiating through my body. I continue to pace, unaware of anything outside of my red-tinted vision. My fingers twitch with the need to use my dagger on more than just the target in my house. I'd love to carve up Alya's picture-perfect face, but honestly, she's just a nuisance. I'd rather leave her to Seraia, since I know she's not a pushover. There may be something I can do, though...

Marius is the primary subject of my ire. That bastard

thinks he can disrespect my Darling Seraia? Put his *hands* on her? Fucking piece of shit; he'll get what's coming to him by my hand.

*Thwunk*

"What's going on? What in the hells?" As I'm gripping the dagger to remove it and circle around, a voice carries across the room. Yanking the dagger from the wood, I spin, blade in hand, to face the threat.

Only, they aren't a threat. Felix had entered my dorm, using the key I'd given him a few days ago. His look of concern melds with a slight hint of fear in his eyes, and I feel bad for startling him. I'm sure I'm not the image of mental stability, but I don't give a fuck right now.

"They've pushed too far, too many times, Felix," I say, continuing the track I've worn on the floor.

"What are you talking about?" He stalks closer to me, no longer afraid. His eyes shine with worry at my anger. When he stops in front of me, he lifts both hands and cups my shoulders. "Talk to me."

"Seraia. Marius and Alya confronted her yesterday. Alya attacked her, Marius let it happen, and then stood as a shield for Alya when Seraia took the upper hand. He disrespected her, telling her when they marry, he'll control her. And then he swung on her; he hit her!"

Felix's eyes bulge wider with every word that slips from my lips. By the end of my explanation, it's more of a growl, but I don't fucking care.

"When did this happen?"

"Yesterday. I saw Seraia sneaking out to breakfast early when I went for a workout. I stopped her and noticed her face was swollen on one side, and she had scratches healing down the other. I insisted she explain, and she told me they finally decided to ambush her."

"Evidently, Seraia's father wants her to cozy up to Marius, but ever since the first time she ran into him with you, she's been getting creeper vibes. Then you two bonded. She fears telling her father, and with no word from her, her father went straight to Marius's dad. Sometime recently, they formed an agreement for betrothal."

"What?! No! She's mine—ours!"

"Exactly what I was thinking. I think I've come up with a plan to cancel this wedding. Are you up for helping me?" I don't care that my words are laced with the fury I've allowed to build. "These fucking bitches are going to learn the hard way not to cross me."

"I'll help, but I'm not too violent. I'll do what I have to, though, for Seraia."

"Don't worry," I say with a dark grin. "I'll do the heavy lifting, so long as you can keep our girl distracted by engaging her in part of this plan. You can't tell her what we're doing, though. Here's what I was thinking..."

MY PLAN WORKED EXACTLY how I'd hoped. I had Felix escort Seraia to her combat course this evening, and as I'd expected, Alya tried her shit again. Except Marius wasn't there to back her up, and Seraia easily handed Alya her ass. I'd watched to ensure it was the distraction I'd hoped for, then I made my way to Alya's dorm.

Considering they had combat class, I had predicted Alya would leave her most prized possession in her room. With a few twists of my wrist, I picked the lock on her door. Her amulet, the treasure I was after, was sitting on display on her desk. I smirked as I lifted the gaudy gem from where it hung and pocketed it before pulling a note from within my glove. I unfolded it and left it in plain sight of where the amulet had hung.

*I can't do this. I don't love you enough to keep you around while I run from this marriage. I don't want Seraia, and to be honest, you are too whiny for me. I can't stand it when you complain so much. So, as payment for all the times I dealt with your shit, this amulet now belongs to me. Thankfully, this will fetch a pretty penny with the traders. I should be able to start my life over far away. Don't come looking for me; it won't end well for you.*

I didn't go home, though. Instead, I turned toward the woods. There, I waited patiently, inspecting my dagger.

About an hour after both suns went down, I finally got my chance. The wolves at the school tended to run together, and tonight was the first night of the full moon, so I knew they would be running as a pack. They all met at one location, one I'd scouted for this entire year. When they returned, that's when I got lucky.

I stay hidden, watching the pack shift and disperse after redressing, but our boy Marius seems a little overconfident, strutting around naked longer than anyone else. I begin to creep forward, sticking to the shadows as everyone else wanders home. It's then that I overhear the conversation.

"Yeah, she has no idea," he says with a smirk to the two remaining shifters getting dressed. "Father set this up, so I'll have to go through with it, unless I find another escape plan. If I have to go through with it, she will be tied to a bed, and I'll fuck her morning and night, until she's pregnant. Then she'll stay a prisoner in my house except for social events. There is no way I'll actually consider a true marriage to that cow."

"But what about friends? Family? How will you convince them that she's okay?" one of the two remaining jackasses asks.

"Oh, I'll drag her with me to events, and we'll visit our family and friends," Marius adds. "She'll be under strict orders to behave, or she'll be chained in a dungeon cell whenever we return home."

"That's cruel, bro," the other imbecile chimes in.

"I don't fucking care," Marius says. "She's there only for me to impregnate. As soon as that happens, I won't have to touch her again. And with any luck, a healthy baby will be born, and I can kick her to the curb for cheating on me because by then, I'll be able to show her mate mark without anyone questioning it. If she has one and I don't, then I can say the bitch isn't my mate, and she fucked someone else."

I don't know how long it takes for these idiots to finish dressing, but as Marius walks off in one direction, the other two head the opposite way. I begin to stalk my prey, knowing I don't have much time before he reaches the dorms.

Quickly formulating a plan, I project my aura in front of Marius to confront him.

"Marius Kelridge," I say, humor lining my words, "and just what do you think you are doing, talking about my girl like that?"

"What?! Who are you? What do you want?!" he shrieks.

"Well, I was just going to beat you up a bit, maybe disfigure you a little. But now, after what I just overheard, I'm rethinking my generosity."

"Gen-generosity?" Marius's face pales to a ghostly white in the moonlight as he stutters like a small child.

"Yes," I say calmly. "I was just going to chop off your dick, because your goal of having children would've been moot. But now, since you think you can abuse the love of my life, hold her prisoner, and fuck her without her expressed permission, I think a little premortem dismemberment is in order."

"Wha-what?" Gods, his fucking nervous stutters are getting on my nerves.

As my projection continues to talk, I creep up behind Marius and kick out his knee from the side before falling on top of him and breaking his elbow as well. His screams of pain aren't nearly to the level I want them, but I'm going to have to engage in a silencing spell.

Since he's incapacitated, I recite the spell, creating a perimeter for me to work within. I begin circling him as he lies protecting his side with two broken limbs; that's okay, I can match up the symmetry for him. I rush up, spin him to his belly, and then pop his other knee. This time his screams become panicked, and a grin spreads across my face. Now time to decide—should I break his other elbow? Or collarbone? No, elbow for symmetry, for sure.

Once I've completely broken all of his limbs, I pull out my lovely dagger. "See this? This right here is my baby, Devina. She's always done right by me, and I know she's not going to fail me tonight. Are you, baby?" I turn the dagger around, kissing the flat of the blade.

"Devina is going to help me punish you. First, I'm going to start by slicing your jaw muscles. Then I'm going to reach in and cut out your tongue. That's for talking bad about my Darling. Then I'm going to start by removing each of your fingers, then your thumbs, then your hands. And that will be for *daring to touch her.*

"After that, I'll probably remove your toes and then your feet. No real reason; I guess just because I want to cause you pain. And if you're still alive after that, I'll work my way up your body. It's simple, really."

"What the fuck, man?!" Marius wails. "Are you psychotic?"

"Possibly. I guess that's a lesson you learned just a little too late, huh?" and with that little quip, I start in. His screams quickly turn into gurgles as I slice those jaw muscles; I can't have him biting me, can I? The red mist that sprays into the night draws a smile to my face as my fun really begins.

I lose track of time as I play with my prey, bathing in the blood of my Darling's enemy. I do notice his screams taper off sometime after I sever his left palm from his wrist. It doesn't stop me, though. I continue on, separating his digits and limbs from his body. He doesn't deserve a formal dragon burial ceremony, so I'm going to ensure these parts find their way across Naesala.

I'd do anything to exact vengeance for her, and tonight, Marius Kelridge found out just how far I'd go.

SERAIA

"**G**ods, I can't get enough of you," Felix murmurs into my neck as I fumble to unlock my dorm door. His hands paw at my ass, and desire flares through my core as I feel his body press up against mine. My mate feels so gods damned good, and after this morning's chaos, I'm ready to spend some time with him and our boyfriend.

*Our boyfriend.* I love that so much. These men adore me, and I love how well they take care of me. Like this morning, Irik called Felix and me to come to the dining hall for a surprise. Turns out, Alya was there, throwing the biggest tantrum I've ever seen, upending chairs and tossing plates of food across the room. She still looked pretty worse for wear after the beat down I served yesterday because of her attitude. I swear, this chick has issues.

This morning, she was going on about losing her amulet. Something about Marius being a lying, useless coward, and now her amulet was gone. Her dad was bound to make her return home, because she lost her family heirloom. Her father, King Noru Caldero, was reportedly a vicious ruler of his people. This, unfortunately for her, didn't exempt his own daughter.

As I watched the spectacle Alya displayed, my song awoke, and I glanced over at Felix. He seemed to feel the same thing because he turned to face me, and the surprised look on his face matched mine.

The moment Irik stepped up behind us, I immediately tasted a wave of his lust. "I think we should... leave," he said. "I wouldn't want her to turn her ire your way." That pretty much sealed our decision to make our way toward my dorm, that flame of lust from Irik only growing larger and more potent.

At this point, I'm barely able to contain myself. I finally unlock the door, barreling through and allowing the guys to follow me. Half-jogging all the way to my bed, I spin, my eyes locking in on Irik as he and Felix step into the room behind me. Gods, those two are so fucking hot.

Irik smirks at me before he yanks Felix and shoves him against the back of the closed door. The 'oomph' of surprise from Felix makes me giggle, which draws his attention.

"Just you wait, Baby," he croons as Irik kisses up his neck and along his jaw. Irik soon finds Felix's lips, and while the kiss is urgent and needy, there is a hint of sweetness there. I see it as Irik drags his hands up Felix's chest before he runs them up over his shoulders to cup his neck. When Felix grinds his hips forward into Irik's, Irik smirks at him and stops. He leans in, whispers something into Felix's ear, and then both men turn their fiery gazes in my direction. *Did I hear Irik say 'fuck me'?*

"Darling," Irik hums as he advances on me, Felix right

behind him. "I think it's about time we got rid of your clothes."

"Oh, that's exactly what I was thinking," Felix chimes in. He moves in behind me, reaching down to grab the hem of my sundress and lifting it over my head. The temperature difference between his warm hands as they skim over my body and the coolness of the room causes goosebumps to cover my skin.

"That's our girl; so willing to allow us to worship you, aren't you, Darling?" Irik whispers sweet words into my ear before he drops to his knees in front of me. His rough hands stir my song as they trace over my breasts and soft curves. They hook into my panties, and as he begins to tug them down, he glances up at me with mischief in his eyes. "Handsome, I think we should show our girl a good time. What do you think?"

"Mmm, sounds like fun to me," Felix says as he steps aside and reaches a hand out to me, tugging me back onto the bed while Irik crawls up from the floor. His slow and languid movements make me feel like I'm his prey, and he's about to devour me.

As Irik settles between my legs, he pushes one of my thick thighs back and to the side, leaning over to inhale a breath from my center. The groan that rumbles from his chest sparks a fire within me, and I need more. He seems to know this, though, because he beckons Felix to him.

Felix strips off his shirt and shoes before joining us on the bed. He mimics the pose Irik takes, spreading my other thigh up and back, exposing my glistening core. A shuddering breath escapes me when he strokes a finger through my folds.

"You are so fucking beautiful. I can't believe you are ours," he says before leaning in and licking the length of my center. When he pulls back, he looks up at Irik as he circles his arm around my thigh. As Felix begins to circle his coarse fingertips around my clit, Irik tilts his head and watches my core clench around nothing from Felix's attention.

"So needy, aren't you, Darling? How about I help you out?" With a swift thrust, he pushes one finger inside me, before pulling all the way out and adding another. I can't help but pant as these two men worship my body, elevating me higher and higher.

"Yes," I moan out loud. Looking down, I watch as they lean forward into a kiss. Slowly and sensually, they share a moment while driving me deeper into ecstasy. I almost explode when they move down to kiss and tongue my clit together. Felix moves his hand to balance before shifting to add his other hand in with Irik's. Fuck, both of them. Both of their fingers. Four fucking fingers; oh my gods.

I'm right there; right on the precipice of coming when Irik pulls back, stopping Felix as well. *Fuck.* Fuck him. Damnit. I lean up, staring wild-eyed at them both, only their knowing smirks shining back at me.

"Sit up, Baby. I need you to ride me," Felix growls. I do as he says, and he switches with me, stripping off his pants and settling into my spot on the bed. Swinging my leg over him, I settle across his hips. His dick is hard and ready for me, but I grind over him for a minute, relishing the feel of his cock gliding through my folds before I lift up and sink down over him. Fucking hells, he's so thick. The stretch is always a bit at first until my body adjusts.

I begin to move, pivoting my hips and bouncing on my knees. It takes a few minutes before we both realize Irik has stripped down and joined us. His hand skates over my ass as he crawls up to kneel by Felix's head.

"Handsome, I'm going to need you to open your

mouth." Irik's dirty words have me squirming, clenching my core as I grow close again. This time, I'm on top, so I don't have to stop. I keep going, and as Felix takes Irik's cock in his mouth, Irik throws his head back. "Fuck, your lips feel so good wrapped around my dick."

When he looks up, he turns to me, staring at my body as I fuck Felix. He reaches over and gathers my hair in one hand before pulling my lips to his. This feels so fucking amazing! My syren is reaching out, caressing Felix's while we both drink in Irik's desire for us. He releases my hair and grazes his hand down my back before cupping an ass cheek. He breaks our kiss before looking into my eyes.

"Has anyone gone here, Darling?" he asks as he trails a finger down the center of my ass. I gasp, not used to the sensation.

"No," I say breathlessly.

"I'd like to try, one day. Can I touch you here?"

"Y-yes," I say as my legs begin to shake.

Leaning over, I offer Irik better access. This, fortunately, also brings me face-to-face with Felix laving Irik's dick. *Why, thank you, I think I will join you.* Jumping in with Felix, I run my tongue along the side of Irik's cock. Felix has warmed the little silver barbells with his own mouth, so they feel like a warm massage on my tongue.

When Irik grips Felix's hair, ripping himself from both of our mouths and instead sliding deep into Felix's throat, causing him to gag and moan, I explode. I try to keep moving, but I think somewhere in my bliss, I fall, and Irik slowly helps me to lie on Felix's chest.

When I return to earth, Irik has already moved behind me between Felix's legs. "Come on, Darling," he whispers. "Lift up so Felix can slide out. I want to take you from behind."

I sit up and lean to the side, Felix quickly shifting and pulling his rock hard dick from me, leaving me feeling empty. When I groan with his movements, he chuckles, but still turns to provide me with a pillow. The extra height lifts my hips, showing off my swollen pussy to Irik, who instantly takes advantage of the open access.

He leans down, swiping his tongue through my seam. I buck at the unexpected thrill as a shiver runs down my spine. He chuckles and notches the blunt tip of his cock at my entrance. That chuckle falls away, transforming into a groan as he sinks into my cunt. I gasp as each piercing hits right over my g-spot.

I'm lost in the sensations he's providing me, the haze of pleasure only clearing when Irik stops. Lifting my head to look back, my eyes widen when I find Felix bending Irik over me.

Oh my fucking gods.

Felix will be fucking Irik into me in mere moments. Just the thought of that image has my syren on edge and my walls spasming. Irik grips tightly to my hip as Felix prepares to enter him, and when Irik bites down gently on my shoulder, I realize this is happening.

"Fuck," Felix gasps. "You feel so fucking good, sir." The formal address catches my attention, but I assume that's something they worked out between them.

Then all hell breaks loose. Felix begins to fuck Irik, who in turn pounds into me, and I fly so high with the combined emotions and desires that I fear the suns will burn me. I have no idea how long this lasts because once I crest that peak, my climax rolls from one to another.

"Darling, fuck," Irik pants. "Felix, oh my gods, you feel so fucking good, and Seraia is about to strangle my dick. Fuck, fuck, fuck," he curses as he comes, groaning as he drains himself deep inside my core. He struggles to not slump against me, but Felix begins to chase his own orgasm, and the breaths that echo through the room put me at peace. I'm so thankful that Felix and I found someone who loves us both.

Felix comes a moment later with a roar, finally spent. He gently withdraws from Irik before falling onto the bed beside me. I can feel his syren's song, joyful and satisfied. What I don't realize, though, is that Irik disappeared.

When I roll over to move the pillow, I spot him exiting my bathroom with a washcloth. He smiles, a sweet gesture I rarely see from him. I return the smile, just in time for him to throw the washcloth at Felix, who jumps in surprise.

Felix immediately uses the washcloth to clean between my legs, and my heart swells with the tenderness. As he's finishing, Irik climbs onto the bed behind me, wrapping his arm around my waist.

"Darling," he says softly, "we have a gift that symbolizes our commitment to you. I can't publicly claim you, and I know neither your father nor the Thalassian law will recognize me. Felix will always be the one to stand by your side, and he was critical to us being able to gift this to you. This is to prove that together, we will overcome anything."

Irik reaches over my head, dangling a bright red, nine-pointed star amulet in front of me. I gasp when I recognize it.

"You stole it from her?" I ask, shocked and unsure if I should accept it.

"Yes. She owed you for the disrespect she's shown you from day one. This is supposedly from the fires of Thisavroś, with ancient power imbued inside. I'm going to dedicate my life to finding a way to harness its power for you."

Well then. I can't reject it, with all it symbolizes. "If you want to be an advisor when I become Premier, then I'd like for you to harness that power for yourself. You can use it to help me build my homeland. If you're willing to join us?" My hopeful tone must break his heart, because he lowers his head, taking my lips with his.

"Darling," he whispers into my mouth, "I'll never leave you. The fates put us together, whether or not they chose to bestow me a mark. You'll never lose me. Neither of you."

# AFTERWORD

I hope you could appreciate this story for what it is. This was only a hint at a part of Terranea University's past, and the events that happen here lead to the story told in the main books of the series. While I've heard feedback that readers wished they knew more of this trio's story, the main point was to show that Seraia found her mate. She would leave a legacy with her descendants that would lead to important events in the future. Irik's role also was a key aspect in this legacy, and while Seraia has children, none are fathered by Irik. His role was different than Felix, and this will be explained in later books.

Just know that these three got their happily ever after, the way it fit them.

# ALSO BY NATASHA PIERCE

**Titans of Terranea**

*A dark, paranormal why choose romance*

The Seduction in Starlight

The Illusions of Innocence

**Pierced By Darkness**

*A dark, paranormal anthology*

*(Out of print)*

**Things Get Dark**

*A dark Halloween anthology*

Things Get Dark

**Scandalous Slopes**

*A dark, sports why choose romance*

Escaping the Cold

Frost Bitten

Dark Winter

# About the Author

Natasha Pierce is the pen name for a book-obsessed wife and mom of three rambunctious boys. She has always been a fan of escaping into the fantastical word of fiction, but never thought she'd be able to write anything, let alone full books. She soon found the Indie book community, and with the support of all of the friends she's made, when the idea for her(hopefully first of many) series came to her, she's been able to slowly develop into a writer. Natasha will be branching out to various sub genres of romances books, however they will all have either dark elements or a why choose aspect to the romance. She hopes to be able to continue to share the stories in her head with the world.

Natasha lives in the Tampa Bay, Florida area. She is a fan of watching hockey, and enjoys reading and fishing.

This is Natasha's sixth book.

facebook.com/natashapierceauthor

instagram.com/natashapierceauthor

tiktok.com/@natashapierce_author

amazon.com/author/natashapierce

bookbub.com/profile/natasha-pierce

goodreads.com/natashapierce

pinterest.com/natashapierceauthor

threads.net/@natashapierceauthor

www.ingramcontent.com/pod-product-compliance
Lightning Source LLC
Chambersburg PA
CBHW051244160726
47994CB00003B/1016